ORIGINS

Adapted by Ned Lerr

Based on the Disney Interactive Studios videogame

Original concept by Fil Barlow and Helen Maier

DISNEP PRESS

New York

ORIGINS

CHAPTER ONE

Rallen and Jeena walked into the briefing room at Nanairo Planetary Patrol headquarters on planet Kollin with their usual calm demeanor, but they were not prepared to encounter the menace that awaited them.

Jeena saw it first. As soon as Rallen observed his partner's eyes widen, he followed her gaze. Ten meters away he saw what appeared to be an enormous, vicious, green-and-black plantlike creature, with razor-sharp yellow spikes. Although neither of them had ever seen a Krawl quite like it, everything about it shrieked *Krawl*.

Without hesitation, Rallen threw out his right arm to protect Jeena, while raising his left arm and preparing to summon the Spectrobes, the mysterious creatures who were the enemies of these creatures of the dark.

"Wait!"

Rallen froze and Jeena jumped. They turned to see their chief, Commander Grant, enter the room. A tall, solidly-built man with steel-gray hair, he seemed the very personification of authority.

Neither Jeena nor Rallen snapped to attention, as they would normally have done. "Sir," they said in unison, both keeping their eyes securely on the Krawl.

"At ease," the commander said, pointing a device at the Krawl. There was an audible click, and the creature disappeared. "Merely a

hologram," he
explained. "Thought
it might prove useful for
today's briefing. Given your
reaction, however"—his lips
twitched into an almost smile—"perhaps it's
best to avoid the visual aids for now. Besides,
after speaking with Aldous and learning some
new information about the Krawl, I think we'll
have enough to deal with."

The room quickly began filling up with other
members of the NPP. Jeena and Rallen said hello
to some, waved to others, but when it came time
to find seats, they did so together. Funny, Jeena
thought, how facing grave times can bond people
together.

In the front row, Jeena and Rallen saw their
two new friends: Aldous, the old man who intro-
duced them to the Spectrobes, and Professor

Kate, the scientist who helped them unlock the Ancient ship on planet Nessa. Rallen smiled in their direction, and Aldous and Professor Kate politely waved back.

Commander Grant strode to the podium at the front of the room. All talking ceased immediately.

"The rumors you've heard are true," he said. "We are facing an enemy the likes of which we've never encountered before. It is called the Krawl, and it is an extinction-level event. Already, this grim juggernaut has laid waste to countless civilizations, vaporizing entire planets. Its leader has so far successfully eluded all detection. All we have is a name: *Krux*."

The silence gave way to an excited hubbub. Commander Grant allowed it to continue for a few seconds, then raised his hand. The room grew quiet again. "The Krawl are a deadly enemy, genetically designed for one purpose and one purpose only—and that is to kill. It must never be underestimated. It is on the move. It is strong. BUT." The commander paused, then said firmly, "It *can* be beaten. It *has* been beaten before. And it *will* be beaten again. By us."

After the briefest of moments, the room exploded in raucous cheers. Rallen and Jeena looked at each other and smiled.

"Piece of cake," Rallen said with a grin.

Jeena shook her hand and laughed. "You *did* hear the part about them vaporizing entire planets, yes?"

Before Rallen could reply, Commander Grant turned to the two officers. "Rallen. Jeena. If you would?"

They both looked up guiltily. But Commander Grant didn't look angry or annoyed—not that he often did. He had stepped back from the podium and was now gesturing toward it. Rallen knitted his eyebrows together until Jeena stood up and motioned for him to do the same. "Come on," she whispered. "He wants us up there."

The look of panic that crossed Rallen's face almost caused Jeena to burst out laughing, but he got up—a bit slower than usual—and followed his partner up to the front of the room.

They both stood at attention. "At ease," Commander Grant said crisply. "As you've had the most experience—at least recently—with the Krawl, it might be helpful for your fellow officers to briefly hear from two of their own just what we're up against."

Jeena nodded and waited for Rallen to begin. When the silence grew awkwardly long, she looked over at Rallen and was shocked to see he was staring at her expectantly. "You sure?" she asked quietly. His smile conveyed perfectly just how sure he was.

All right then, Jeena thought, and she stepped up to the podium. "Good morning," she said.

"Most of you have heard rumors about what Commander Grant just spoke about. I don't know exactly what those rumors are, so I'm just going to very briefly run down what I know for a *fact* to be true." Jeena's tone became very demure.

"First off, as the commander said, we're up against something called the Krawl. Krawl vary in shape, size, and appearance. They can adapt to their environment and use it to their advantage. But in general, most are approximately five meters tall, extremely fast, deadly, and dedicated to wiping out anything in their path. And they have the ability to devour entire planets. . . . Any questions?"

The room burst into a low chatter. Jeena scanned the sea of shocked and horrified faces as everyone tried to cope with what she had just told them. She turned to Commander Grant with a concerned look on her face. Did I say too much? she wondered. Commander Grant stepped back up to the podium and gave a little cough into the microphone to get the group's attention. Immediately, the room was dead silent again.

Jeena continued. "I know how you all must feel," she said. "I felt the same way when we first encountered the Krawl. In fact, I still do." She smiled, and many of the officers chuckled softly, helping release the tension in the room. Rallen smiled as well. Wow, he thought. She's good.

"There's also the High Krawl. As the name implies, they're more sophisticated than the Krawl—much more. They're . . ." She hesitated and glanced over at Commander Grant. The look he gave her indicated it might be best to skip over any more details, since most of the room was still recovering from her last bit of information. "Actually, let's move on. Now, I know this is a lot to take in at once," she said sympathetically. "And I know it sounds somewhat overwhelming. That's because it is." She smiled, and several of the officers smiled back, if rather grimly. "But I haven't told you about how we might be able to stop this threat and bring peace back to the Nanairo Galaxy." Jeena smiled proudly. "The *Spectrobes*!"

There was a long pause. A few whispers could be heard in the audience. One officer quietly mentioned how he had heard that Jeena kept giant pet monsters in her ship. Another stated that he saw Rallen with a massive green and blue beast within the hills of Tabletop Mountain. Everyone else was confused. Jeena turned back to her partner and looked worried. Rallen motioned for her to keep going.

Turning back to the audience, Jeena flashed another big smile. "Actually, *Rallen*, my *partner*, should probably take over at this point."

Rallen's head jerked up in surprise. She isn't serious . . . is she? he thought.

He saw that she had backed away from the

podium, as though making room for him. So, yes, apparently she was serious.

Rallen felt a little betrayed, but the warm smile on Jeena's face told him it would be okay. Well, he thought, taking a deep breath, here goes nothing.

Rallen grabbed both sides of the podium and then crossed his arms, unsure where to put his hands. Everyone could tell this was not something Rallen was comfortable with. Finally calming down, he placed his hands in his pockets.

"Hey, hi, how are you," he said by way of introduction. "I'm, uh . . . Rallen. But I guess most of you already know that." He paused. He didn't sound confident like Jeena. He tried again. "Right. So . . . the Spectrobes. The Spectrobes are, like, these . . . *creatures*, I guess you'd say. They're pretty small at first. But when you feed them minerals they get bigger, and they're really good fighters when they're adults—like, *really* good," he said, loosening up. He began using his hands and becoming more animated. "And then they become, uh, evolved, when you feed them evolved minerals, and then they're just *awesome*! And sometimes they're fossils, and they're buried, and only a Child Spectrobe can find them. And then you dig 'em up. And then you need a Spectrobe Master to make them not be fossils anymore."

He stopped for breath. Scanning the listeners, he saw puzzlement on their faces, mixed with some skepticism. Rallen glanced over at Jeena, who smiled encouragingly. He appreciated her loyalty, but he knew he wasn't doing as well as she had. He wasn't even sure where to go from here.

"So . . . these Spectrobe things have Masters? Who are they?" said an officer in the audience.

"Well . . ." Rallen said slowly. "I, uh . . . I am. I mean, I'm one of them."

The room was completely silent for one long, painful moment. And then everyone exploded into laughter. Everyone except Rallen and Jeena, that is. Even Commander Grant was smiling as he stepped forward. "Thank you, Jeena. And thank you, Spectrobe Master." The listeners laughed again. "I think that's about as good a point to end as we'll find. Dismissed."

Rallen stared at the floor as the room emptied out. When they were alone again, Rallen stood at attention as he faced the commander. "I could have shown them a Spectrobe! I could have . . . they wouldn't have laughed if—"

Commander Grant silently raised an eyebrow. "Yes, I know, Rallen. But I said at the beginning that I wanted this to be brief. What are the chances of that happening if you'd actually shown them, say, Zozanero? Or the blue and gold Spectrobe beast, Optoger?"

Rallen and Jeena looked at each other. "Zozanero or *who*, sir?" Jeena asked.

"What? Oh, yes, well . . ." Commander Grant said, shaking his head. "Never mind that now. The point is, what would have happened if a Spectrobe had suddenly made an appearance?"

Rallen nodded. "Point taken, sir."

"Good," Commander Grant said. "Now we've received reports of the Krawl regrouping in greater numbers than we've yet seen. There's an anomaly emanating from Sector W. I need you to check it out immediately."

Jeena interrupted. "Sir, with all due respect, that's a remote, low-priority sector."

"We are not taking any chances, is that understood?" Commander Grant said with authority.

Jeena snapped to attention. "Yes, sir!"

With that, the two officers were out the door in a flash.

* * *

*F*ive minutes later, Rallen and Jeena were ready to climb aboard their ship. Maxx, the chief mechanic of the Nanairo Planetary Patrol, was unhappy, as usual.

"Barely had time to give her even two goings-over, and you're already taking her," she grumbled. "I can't guarantee she's ready." But the way Maxx ran her hand over the ship as she spoke made clear the real reason for her displeasure: there was no other ship like her in the fleet, and Maxx never got anywhere near as much time with her as she'd like.

"Are you kidding?" Rallen said. "One quick check from you is better than three checks from anyone else."

Maxx waved him off dismissively, but she didn't turn her head quickly enough to hide the smile breaking out across her face.

"Besides," Rallen added slyly, "I'll be flying.

You know there's no problem I can't handle."

"Yeah, yeah, yeah," Maxx replied. "Get going, flyboy. Just bring her back in one piece. How many pieces you come back in yourself is optional." Turning, Maxx gazed at the Ancient ship from planet Nessa that sat in the background. "Besides, I'll have my hands full until you return."

Jeena and Rallen ran through their preflight checklist.

Everything appeared in perfect order, and minutes later the ship took off in its unique, avian way and they broke free of Kollin's atmosphere.

"Okay," Jeena said, glancing at their location monitor. "We're approaching Sector W. We should be seeing—"

"That?" Rallen asked.

Jeena looked up to see what he was talking about. It resembled one of the cyclones that heralded the arrival of the Krawl, although this one was dark purple at the edge, had a brilliant white light in the center, and was much, much bigger than they expected.

"That's not what I think it is, is it?" Jeena asked, as lightning shot out from the vortex.

"Not sure," Rallen said. "Let's get in a bit tighter and find out."

"Wait," she replied. "Does it look sort of like a portal, or something? Maybe we should—"

"Hello," Rallen said loudly, his surprise audible. "We're getting pulled in. Maybe I can—"

He never got the chance to finish. The ship was soon sucked into the unusual vortex and disappeared.

CHAPTER TWO

*J*eena stopped gripping the arms of the co-pilot's seat and opened her eyes. "Well, *that* was weird."

Rallen looked over at Jeena. "You ever do anything like that before?"

Jeena glared at him. "Get sucked into a black hole? No, Rallen, I can't say I have."

Rallen checked out the view on the monitors. "Was that really a black hole?"

Jeena sighed. "No. If it were, there's a good chance much of planet Kollin might be in here with us. And . . ."

Her fingers flew over the various keyboards and controls. "It's safe to say it's not. In fact, I don't know if you've noticed yet, but Nessa's not with us, either. Or Genshi. Or Himuro. Or any of the other planets in the Nanairo Galaxy."

"What?" Rallen looked skeptical. "How is that possible?"

Jeena shrugged. "Got me. But look around. Recognize any of these constellations?"

Rallen glanced at the monitors, then began to study them more carefully. "Hmm. I don't recognize anything" he said finally.

"Yeah," Jeena agreed.

"We, uh . . . we're in another . . . what? System? Galaxy? Universe? *Dimension?*"

Jeena shook her head slowly. "I don't know."

"Got a guess?"

She frowned. "Well . . . I'd guess probably not universe, and almost certainly not dimension, since so far it seems consistent with our laws of physics. So . . . system, at least. But I don't know. I haven't had a whole lot of experience with other systems. You?"

"Nope. None."

Jeena bit her lip. "Well, first let's see if we can raise the NPP."

She tried to contact headquarters but gave up quickly. "Nothing. Not even a blip."

"Well, that's working," said Rallen, pointing to a monitor on the ship's dashboard. "We're getting a distress signal."

Turning some dials, Jeena focused in on the call.

"Hello! Hello! This is an urgent distress call from planet Wyterra! Please respond! We're under attack by a massive army of Kra—!"

The distress signal broke off into crackling.

Jeena and Rallen looked at each other.

"Do you think they're talking about what I

think they're talking about?" Rallen asked.

Suddenly, the signal came back again.

". . . Survivors . . . Taken shelter . . . The old ruins. Vastly outnumbered . . . Cannot hold out! Please . . . Send help!"

They exchanged worried glances.

"Sounds bad," Rallen said.

"Only one way to find out. Let's track it," Jeena stated. "Not like we have any better options."

They followed the distress signal to a planet that was lush and green, with deep blue skies and wispy white clouds. Although the terrain was hilly, the rises were gentle, and Rallen was able to set the ship down easily. "I see being in some alternate galaxy hasn't impaired your skills," Jeena said.

Rallen grinned. "You don't have to keep being nice to me. I know I'm a lousy public speaker. Just like I know I'm an absolutely awesome pilot. Now are my killer abilities going to all be wasted? Are we about to get poisoned when we go out there?"

Jeena rolled her eyes. "As if. While you were busy bragging, I checked the atmosphere. It's virtually identical to what we've got on the various Nanairo planets."

"Excellent," he said, getting up. "So we're good to go."

Jeena unbuckled. "I'm not sure I'd say that just yet," she said, as they headed for the door.

"Hey, Jeena. I think you should take this," Rallen said abruptly, handing her a gauntlet similar to the one he wore on his wrist, which stored his laser sword.

Jeena took the gauntlet and studied it for a few seconds. "What's this for?"

"Just in case . . . you know . . ." he said, trying to find the right words.

He didn't need to. "Thanks," she said.

"Don't mention it. But remember, I'm the hero. So if there is any danger, you let me handle it. Okay? Okay!" he flashed a big smile and made his way to the ship's back door. Jeena rolled her eyes. She knew a punch line was on its way.

They exited the ship very carefully, each slowly taking in a deep breath of the air. Jeena checked her kaylee; although the handheld computer appeared to be functioning well, it was no more successful at connecting with headquarters than the computer on the ship had been.

"Huh. That's weird. Place looks perfectly fine," Rallen said.

Jeena nodded. "Yeah. But that signal definitely originated from right around here somewhere." A movement caught her attention, and she looked up to see the Child Spectrobe Komainu running off.

"Rallen!" Jeena called. He'd been inspecting

the ship but whipped around immediately.

"Hey!" he called after the Spectrobe. "What are you . . . Jeena, we've got to go get him!"

Jeena started. "Are you sure? I mean, I guess we have to, but I'm not sure immediately running around a planet we've never even heard of before is such a great idea."

"I'm sure you're right," he agreed as he began to run after Komainu. "But I'm also not sure we have a choice."

Jeena sighed and stowed her kaylee, then began to sprint after her comrades.

First Komainu and then Rallen disappeared over a hill. When Jeena crested it, she almost slammed into Rallen, who had come to a stop. "What on—" she said, which was followed by a sudden, "*Oh!*"

Spread out before them were ruins—an immense site. And in the middle of the ruins were something very familiar to them—Krawl.

"Lovely," Jeena said. "We don't know where we are or how we really got here or how we're going to get back. But the Krawl? *That's* the one thing familiar from home."

Rallen grinned. "Now at least I guess we know why Komainu took off like that. Well, looks like that's my cue." He sprinted down the hill, letting out a war cry as he ran. Jeena had to shake her head admiringly. Rallen could be unbearably arrogant and annoying, but he seemed virtually fearless—except when it came to public speaking, of course. Despite the unnaturalness of the move, Jeena ventured closer to the action. Not being a Spectrobe Master herself, there was little she could do to fight the Krawl, but she wanted to be near enough to provide some sort of tactical assistance if needed.

Rallen halted a dozen meters away from the closest Krawl. "Ah, nothing like a little taste of home," he said. He touched the Prizmod. "Let's do this! *Iku ze!*"

Nothing happened.

Rallen looked down at the Prizmod, the device that held the Spectrobes, in surprise. Had he done something wrong?

He tried again. But still no result.

He shook his arm and tried a third time. Still nothing. "What's wrong with this thing?"

"Rallen!"

Rallen looked up just in time to see the Krawl swinging a massive tentacle. He dived away and rolled into a backward somersault.

Jeena cupped her hands around her mouth. "Run!" she yelled.

 Rallen hesitated. "Run!" Jeena yelled again. This time he did.

Jeena ran toward the center of the ruins, and Rallen moved to join her. They now ran side by side. "The Prizmod isn't working! Neither is my shield!" he cried.

"I know!" she replied. "I could tell. I didn't think you were just trying to bluff them."

Rallen grinned. "Ha! Very funny!"

He looked back over his shoulder. Most of the Krawl had stayed where they were, but the one Rallen had tried to engage was following them, and quckly. "We've got a stalker," he said.

Jeena looked back, then nodded her head toward something a little ahead of them. Rallen followed her gaze. "Good idea," he said.

Jeena thought about slowing down slightly, but the Krawl was already faster than they were, and it didn't seem to be losing interest in the chase. In a matter of moments they were at their destination: a small, flimsy temporary bridge apparently made of some sort of organic material.

It stretched about a dozen meters across a ravine. She forced herself not to hesitate and ran across it as fast as she could, refusing to look down until she was nearly there. When she did look down, her stomach seemed to drop into her feet; the chasm was far deeper than she'd anticipated. "Don't look down! Don't look down!" she yelled. Two more steps and her feet were back on solid ground.

"Why not?" Rallen called back. Then, obviously having disregarded her advice, he looked down. "Whoa! Are you *crazy*!?"

Rallen took five more steps at top speed and then jumped forward, spinning around in midair. He landed safely next to Jeena. The Krawl had followed them onto the thin bridge, but it had now slowed down considerably. Already halfway across, it seemed to be having second thoughts about the wisdom of its plan. The force of Rallen's jump had set the entire bridge shaking violently. The Krawl took one more step forward, and due to its mass and the impact of Rallen's jump, the bridge suddenly snapped. The Krawl's tentacles reached out for something to hold. But there was nothing.

"Well, that was exciting," Jeena said, dusting herself off.

Rallen nodded. "Good call on the bridge."

Jeena shrugged. "Seemed logical in the one-point-two seconds I had to debate it internally."

They looked around. "What now?" Rallen asked.

"Go find your rebel Spectrobe, I guess."

Komainu peeked around a corner, then disappeared again. Rallen, exasperated, let out a burst of air and ran. "Bad Komainu!" he called. "Bad boy! Get back here—you hear me?"

"That was very effective, Mister Spectrobe Master," Jeena said.

They saw Komainu head into the mouth of a

cave, and they followed. But they slowed down as it became too dark to see. Rallen felt Komainu brush against his leg. "You're lucky Jeena likes you . . ." Rallen grumbled to the Spectrobe.

Jeena laughed, patting their rogue Spectrobe affectionately. "Don't worry, little guy. He's putty in your hands."

The sound of a pebble being kicked froze them. "Who's there?" came a voice, as a bright light suddenly shone across their faces, from one to the other.

Rallen held a up hand, trying to shield his eyes from the glare. "We're—" he began. But he was cut off by the sound of several people gasping. Then a man whispered, "A *Spectrobe*."

CHAPTER THREE

"**B**wah?" Rallen said.

"Well put," Jeena replied.

A figure stepped forward. He was a bit old and slouched over with a cane in one hand, yet something about him suggested nobility. "It cannot possibly be—can it? As young as you are and yet a full-fledged Spectrobe Master? And it was you who picked up our distress call—thank goodness."

"Yeah . . ." Rallen said slowly. "Can we back

up a bit? Who are you people, and how do you know about the Spectrobes? And while we're at it: where *are* we?"

The man held up a hand. "I am Radese. It was I who sent the distress signal to which—I assume—you have responded. You are on the planet Wyterra, in the Kaio System, and you are the first Spectrobe Master we have seen in many a year. Well . . ." Radese paused, then added, "The first active Spectrobe Master. We are honored and relieved by your presence."

Rallen attempted to look modest. "I understand. I get that a lot."

Jeena rolled her eyes and whispered to Rallen. "You've gotten that exactly once. Nessa was the first time, and, I have to admit, I expected it to be the last time."

Radese watched this with interested but polite eyes. "Ahem. Time is short, and there is much to do. Have you discovered yet that your Prizmod does not work in our system?"

Rallen shook his head. "You know, I'm going to stop wondering how you know all this stuff and just roll with everything. So, yes. I have very much discovered it. What's up with that?"

"That is a long and very complicated answer. For now, simply accept that it is."

"Okay," Rallen said agreeably. "I'm getting good at that. What's this?"

Radese had reached into a satchel and produced a small device which he was holding out toward Rallen. "It's called a Cosmolink. It's an ancient tool, handed down through the generations. In the Kaio System, which is where you are now, this is the one absolutely essential tool of the Spectrobe Master. It is similar to a

Prizmod—although there are several differences, some minor, some not. But unlike your Prizmod, this will work in the Kaio System. It will seem alien at first, I suspect, but I believe you will adjust rapidly."

Rallen took the Cosmolink and was not entirely surprised to note that it seemed to fit on his suit as well as the Prizmod had. "Someday I'm going to get answers to all the questions piling up," he muttered. "Okay, so I suppose I'll discover some of the minor changes on my own, but if you could tell me the major ones, that'd really help, you know, keep me alive."

"Of course," Radese agreed. "The most serious one is that the Cosmolink requires a partner."

"Well, sure—I mean, obviously. Even in the Nanairo Galaxy, I need the Spectrobes."

"No, no, no. Of course you need the Spectrobes. But I mean that the Cosmolink requires the Spectrobe Master to have another *human* partner. You must designate a *Co-Master*," Radese said, holding out another Cosmolink.

Jeena had been off to the side, inspecting the runes on the cave wall, but now she turned around. "What's that, now?"

Radese faced her. "If you are to have any chances of besting the Krawl, you must become a Spectrobe Master as well."

"**U**h . . . yeah, no, I don't think so." Jeena waved her hands. "I think you've got the wrong person. Rallen's the Spectrobe Master. Just ask him. I'm the support staff." She shrugged. "Or the brains of the operation. Depending upon who you listen to."

Radese said nothing.

"Okay, look," said Rallen. "Explain this to me. Why does this Cosmolink mean I need a Co-Master?"

"Because the secret of the Cosmolink's unique power lies in its ability to tap into the deep bond of trust that exists between two mind-souls."

"Bond of trust? Mind-souls?" Rallen questioned.

"Correct. To put it another way, it means you'll need to choose for yourself a proven and dependable battle partner. Am I wrong in assuming you already have such a partner with you?"

Rallen looked over at Jeena and said with surprising gentleness, "You can totally do this."

"Listen, thank you—I appreciate the show of support," she replied. "But you don't have to worry about my feelings. I know my strengths. I know what I'm good at, and I'm not going to say there aren't things I'm very good at. But battling giant monsters? It's not really my thing."

"Jeena—"

"Perhaps she's right," Radese interrupted.

"She's not," Rallen replied. Radese blinked in surprise. Rallen's tone of voice was much harsher than he'd be using with Jeena, as his natural tendency to defend his partner kicked in. "Sorry," he said.

Radese bowed slightly. "Why don't we all venture outside? If the Krawl have left for now, we can go to Haven Village, our home. If the young lady continues to feel she's not the correct Co-Master for you, it is possible you will encounter another mind-soul there with whom you will develop the bond of trust."

Jeena had to laugh. "Oh, very subtle."

"Sure," Rallen agreed, "I click with almost everyone."

There was no sign of the Krawl on the outside of the ruins. Radese pointed out various bits of interest to Jeena. She knew he was, in part, attempting to diffuse the tension. She appreciated the gesture—which worked, as she found the brief history lesson fascinating.

Haven Village was not far away. Nor, they discovered when they arrived, were the Krawl.

Rallen and Jeena didn't know what the village normally looked like, but right now it seemed as though the Krawl had done extensive damage.

Without hesitation, Rallen started to run toward the Krawl in the distance, then checked himself, as he realized he was powerless without a partner. He turned to look back at Jeena, who was looking down at the Cosmolink in her hand.

She opened her mouth, but no words came out. Soundlessly, she shook her head, then sighed. "Fine. Let's, as they say, *do this*!" She clipped the Cosmolink to her wrist gauntlet and gave Rallen a slight grin.

Rallen grinned back. "Follow my lead, partner—*iku ze*!"

Both their Cosmolinks began to vibrate. A

bright light shot out from the device and poured up into the sky. When the blinding light faded, there stood a Spectrobe unlike any Rallen and Jeena had ever seen. It was a pinkish color and had large fangs. Its paws were massive, and its razor-sharp claws were gripping the ground as it crouched into a fighting position. It had wings on its back and looked like it weighed a ton. Yet, something was oddly familiar about its appearance. Jeena looked over at Komainu, then back at the new Spectrobe.

"Rallen. It looks like Komainu, but an evolved version, doesn't it?"

Rallen compared the two, then nodded. "You're right! This might be a Komanoto, the one Aldous mentioned to us a while back."

"Whatever its name is, I'm glad he's on our side!" Jeena said. "So now, how do we make him . . . you know, *attack*!"

That was all the Komanoto needed to hear. It

leaped into action and sliced and smashed its way right through one of the nearby Krawl. It slashed its giant claws and cut another Krawl in half, causing it to melt into a puddle of ooze and then disintegrate.

Rallen and Jeena stood in silence for a few seconds, unsure of what to make of their new Spectrobe's sudden attack. Komanoto turned to face Rallen and Jeena. It looked up to the sky and roared so loudly the ground beneath Rallen and Jeena shook. A moment later, it coalesced into a bright light and poured back into the Cosmolink.

Jeena put her hands on her knees and sucked air into her lungs. "So that's what it's like," she said.

"Hey, you were great!"

Jeena looked at him. "Really?"

"Well . . . no, that Spectrobe did all the work. But you were better than I expected. And you probably will be great. You know, someday."

Jeena made a face at him, but didn't have the breath to respond. Finally she said, "If I could move, I'd hit you."

Radese came up, his face glowing. "Magnificent! You two were incredible!"

Jeena sat up and studied him. He was so much more animated than previously. And . . . was he kidding? She couldn't tell.

Rallen had no doubts. "Yeah, and this was just our first time. We get a few more trials under our belts and watch out."

Radese said, "My people were spared. After such an ordeal, however, their spirits will certainly need some seeing to. If you are willing, you two can be of help in that regard. To meet the young heroes who defeated the Krawl would be inspiring for them."

"Uh . . . yeah," Jeena said automatically, "right."

"Absolutely!" Rallen said. "We're more than

happy to do whatever we can. If seeing a mighty warrior—or two—can be of assistance, we're all over that."

Radese touched his forehead with a thumb. Neither Rallen nor Jeena had ever seen such a gesture before, but they got the impression it was a sign of gratitude. "You are brave *and* kind," Radese said. "Go freely about the village. Explore and introduce yourselves. If you travel to Doldogo, perhaps you will encounter Kamtoga— I believe you will find it most enlightening when you do. When you're done, come to my home. It's right at the end of this road."

CHAPTER FOUR

"**S**o? How was it?"

Jeena didn't bother to ask what Rallen was talking about. Instead, she watched some sort of animal search for food. It had six legs and light purple fur, and it poked around the base of a tree. She didn't know the name of the animal. Or the tree. Or anything about their surroundings. For a scientist, this should have been a golden opportunity, but the sheer quantity of things unknown to her was a bit overwhelming.

"It was . . ." she said. "I'm not sure. I mean, it was scary—terrifying, really. And interesting, the way I could make that Spectrobe attack upon my command. The power I felt! It was unlike anything I've ever experienced before."

"So," Rallen replied, "you're saying it was totally awesome."

"Well," she said, shaking her head. Then she stopped and considered. "Yeah. I guess I kinda am."

"That's what I'm talkin' about!" he said, slapping her on the back happily. "See? You didn't think you could do this. I knew you could."

"Hey, I'm still not sure," she said. But even as she spoke, a part of her wondered if she was just being modest.

"Check it out," Rallen said, nodding toward a cave.

Jeena looked at it, then looked around. They'd passed a dozen houses and more than a few fields.

For some reason, this cave stood out. Rallen headed toward it.

"What's up?"

"I dunno," he replied. "Just something about it. You know?"

Jeena understood. She didn't know what it was, but something about the cave felt odd. They stopped just inside its mouth.

"Weird," Rallen said. "This is totally different from the rest of the village."

"Yeah, you're right," Jeena agreed, inspecting one of the walls. "It's like something from the ruins on Nessa."

They poked around for a few minutes. It was clear from the things left lying around that the cave had been used in the past as a house. Jeena saw what appeared to be a sort of footlocker behind a boulder. Carefully, she opened it. Something shiny caught her eye and she picked it up.

"Uh, Rallen?"

"What's up?"

"If you ask me," Jeena said softly, "I'd say we're not the first NPP officers to find this place."

Rallen took the object Jeena was holding up.

"Did you really just find this in there?" Rallen asked.

"Yeah," Jeena replied.

"But . . . it's an NPP badge."

"Yeah."

"What's a Nanairo Planetary Patrol badge doing in a footlocker in a cave on Wyterra?"

"Got me. But obviously we're not the first ones from the Nanairo Galaxy to visit the Kaio System."

Rallen looked at the badge. "This whole thing just keeps getting weirder and weirder." He tucked away the NPP badge. As he did, he felt his kaylee vibrate. Surprised, he pulled it out. "Hey! I think this thing might be working."

"No way," Jeena said, and checking her own kaylee. "You're right!"

Moments later, Commander Grant's visage appeared. "Commander! Can you read me?"

He nodded. "The signal's weak, so let's make this fast. Are you and Rallen all right?"

"We're fine, sir, thanks. You know you can't keep us down. We're fighters," Jeena said with confidence.

"I know," The commander replied. "But even fighters have to be lucky. We've been worried since you two disappeared."

"Us, too, for a while. But then we touched down on a planet called Wyterra," Jeena said.

"You're in the Kaio System?"

"Huh?" Rallen interjected. "Commander Grant, how did you know—?"

"Hmm," Commander Grant muttered. "So you did cross a portal. When we lost contact with you, there was no debris, so I wondered. . . ." The signal faded.

"Sir?" Jeena yelled. "What's that? Please repeat."

The commander's reply was garbled. Jeena tried again, "Commander, I can't chart the coordinates of the Nanairo Galaxy from here for some reason. Commander? Commander!"

The connection broke off. Jeena tried to restore it but finally gave up.

Rallen looked confused. "What he muttered about the portal—you heard that, right? I mean, how'd he know about that?"

"I don't know," she replied. "It's weird. But I'm going to take it as a good sign. Or at least try to."

They exited the cave and started back toward the center of the village.

"So, should we go find this Kamtoga or head toward Radese's?" Jeena asked.

"I don't know," Rallen replied, scratching his head. "How about we just start in this direction and see what happens?"

"Oh, boy," she said. "With our luck? *Something* will. But it won't necessarily be pleasant."

"Who are you? What do you want?" a voice rang out from behind them.

Rallen and Jeena turned in surprise. Their questioner was quite a bit older than they were, although her hair was still thick and a deep orange color, and her blue eyes were piercing. Around her neck hung a gold medallion carved with an intriguing symbol. Her hostility was obvious, but neither Rallen nor Jeena could figure out what she was so angry about.

"Uh, we're . . . friends, I guess, of Radese's?" Rallen replied, unsure how to describe himself.

"Hmm," the woman growled, seeming almost annoyed that the young pair had some excuse to be there. "I don't know you. And I don't like strangers."

"Is that right?" Rallen said, bristling. "How do you like people who fight the Krawl and try to protect your town?"

"What my friend means," Jeena said, stepping

between Rallen and the woman, "is that Radese suggested we meet with someone named Kamtoga— perhaps you could tell us where he or she is?"

The name caught the woman off guard, but only for a moment. "Do I look like Kamtoga's secretary?" the woman asked. She took a closer look at Rallen's badge. "So you're NPP officers, huh?"

"As a matter of fact, we are!" Rallen said cheerfully. "We—"

"A little young, aren't you?" she shot back.

"Well, what can I say? I'm unusually gifted for someone my age. Not to mention charming."

"I don't like charming," the woman said coldly.

"But that's because you've never met me before," Rallen said, determined.

But Jeena interrupted. "So have you known any other NPP officers?"

The woman glared at Jeena. "What's it to you?"

Jeena realized that this woman clearly had no interest in telling them anything they needed to know, but she knew she couldn't give up "So, you don't know where Kamtoga is?" Jeena said sweetly.

The woman grumbled, clearly not eager to tell them how to find Kamtoga. "Probably by the Tree of Life in the forest," she spat out, spinning on her heels and stalking away.

Rallen stuck her tongue out at the woman's back, causing Jeena to laugh.

"Boy, you've got a way with older women," Rallen said.

She nodded. "Can't say the same for you."

CHAPTER FIVE

"*N*o! Stop!"

The moment the cry went up, both Rallen and Jeena reacted . . . but in very different ways. Jeena froze, instinctively going completely silent so she could isolate and locate the direction the sound was coming from, and then analyzing the odds to determine whether it was a sincere plea or merely a trap.

Rallen, on the other hand, sprinted in the direction of the call as fast as he could. Shaking her head, Jeena ran off in pursuit.

Good thing I didn't wait another second, she thought; the forest they were now in was heavily wooded, and it was difficult to see more than a few yards ahead at any time.

Suddenly, she broke into a clearing and saw what she had been afraid they'd find: Krawl.

Strangely, however, there was also a young woman with her back against a huge tree. And she seemed to be facing down the Krawl, which were slowly advancing toward her.

"Back off!" the woman snarled. "You are *not* touching this tree—do you hear me?"

"Wow," Jeena said.

"You can say that again," Rallen replied.

Jeena looked at him in surprise. Was she imagining things or was Rallen maybe a bit . . . smitten with this unusual woman?

There was no time to think about it, Jeena realized. Now that they were both there, it was time for the Spectrobe Master to kick into action. Or, she dimly realized, *Masters*.

"So," she said, "what do you say we do this? *Iku ze!*"

Rallen grinned at her in surprise. "Rock on!"

Concentrating, the two Spectrobe Masters summoned Komonatu. "Care to give it a go?" Rallen asked, gesturing like a gentleman offering the right of way.

"Uh . . ." Jeena said, unsure. "Attack?"

Komonatu stood stone still, growling at the Krawl.

"Come on," Rallen urged. "You gotta really mean it. Do it like you did before."

"Yeah, but before I didn't *mean* to," Jeena said. She concentrated as hard as she could, then said in a voice not quite like any she'd ever used before, "*Go!*"

Komonatu surged forward as though he'd been shot out of a plasma cannon. He hit the enemy below what Jeena guessed was a knee. The Krawl buckled slightly. Jeena and Rallen, working as one, took advantage of the moment, unleashing their laser swords and running forward, Jeena from the left and Rallen from the right.

The Krawl roared and lashed out at them. Jeena fell backward and hit the ground hard, the air rushing out of her. The Krawl moved in for the kill. But as it brought its tentacle down, Jeena raised her sword. Unable to stop its momentum, the Krawl impaled itself.

A flash of light, and all was silent.

"You okay?" Rallen said, helping Jeena to her feet.

"I think I might be sick," Jeena said, trying to catch her breath. "But I'm alive."

The woman was kneeling by the tree, her red hair covering her face. Rallen and Jeena walked toward her uncertainly. Up close, it was obvious the tree was sick.

"What . . . what happened to it?" Rallen asked.

"It was poisoned, thanks to the Krawl and that black fluid that was pouring out of it." She gestured toward the river. "All the water's been tainted. It happened upstream first, then it slowly made its way down here."

Jeena raised her eyebrows. "The Krawl? Are you sure?"

The woman laughed bitterly. "Without a doubt. I've seen it with my own eyes."

Rallen whistled. "You mean you've been *watching* them?"

She nodded. "Of course. This tree . . ." She paused and shook her head. "It's not just any tree. All the water around here passes through it. And when it comes out the other side, it's absolutely pristine."

The woman touched the tree reverently. "It was a gift given to us untold ages ago. We treasure it. This tree is the beating heart of our whole life here. It *is* life to us. And it's an honor to be the one chosen to watch over it."

"I'm so sorry there isn't more we can do to help," Rallen said.

The woman smiled and waved a hand. "Oh, no, you've done more than enough already."

Jeena replied, "But . . . the tree's poisoned."

"Yes," the woman agreed. "It *was* poisoned. But by defeating the Krawl, you two have stopped that from continuing. Now the tree's natural abilities will take over again. Just look at how much better it is already."

Jeena and Rallen looked closer at the tree and were astonished to note that it really did appear considerably healthier and greener than it had been just a few minutes before.

"Whoa . . . that's some life force running through it."

The woman nodded. "This is nothing. It's not even back to full health yet. If you stick around,

you'll see what I mean. And I hope you will."
Jeena noticed that the woman was looking
right at Rallen as she said this. "You were both
incredibly brave," she added. "We're so grateful
to you."

Now it was Rallen's turn to wave a hand
dismissively. "Hey, just doin' our jobs."

"Well," the woman replied, "I believe trees
have emotions, just like we do. It's joyful again
. . . thanks to you."

Jeena turned to Rallen and grabbed his shoulder. "Hey, are you allergic to something? You're
all . . . or wait. Are . . . are you blushing?"

Rallen looked panicked, and he touched a
hand to his cheek, as though to check Jeena's
claim. "What—me? I am not!"

The woman smiled. "So," she said, "what are
a pair of Spectrobe Masters doing here?"

"Boy, this place isn't much like home, is it?"
Rallen said to Jeena. "Everyone knows about the

Krawl and the Spectrobes."

"Mmm," Jeena agreed. "And some of them even *like* Spectrobe Masters." She turned to the woman. "We're looking for someone named Kamtoga."

The woman nodded. "Of course. I'm Salia."

"It's very nice to meet you," Rallen said.

Jeena's mouth dropped open at his tone. She was about to commence some truly merciless teasing when something else caught her attention.

"Wait . . ." Jeena said. "Where'd that door come from?"

CHAPTER SIX

Rallen and Jeena started at the door which had suddenly appeared at the base of the tree. "Huh," he said.

She nodded. "Yeah. So. Shall we?"

The door swung open with ease, as though it had been used many times before. Entering it, the officers found themselves going down a dark, winding passage.

"So," Jeena said, "we're somewhere under the Tree of Life."

"Yeah," Rallen agreed.

"Which means Salia could be directly above us right this very moment."

Rallen didn't reply. Jeena tried not to laugh and mainly succeeded.

"Shut up," Rallen said pleasantly.

"What? Me? I didn't say anything," Jeena replied.

"Uh-huh. I heard you very clearly not saying anything."

The passageway suddenly branched out into a large room. Rallen held up his lamp so they could see better.

"Hey," he said. "Pictographs, like in caves and stuff."

Jeena inspected the walls. "Check out this one. Tell me that doesn't look exactly like a Spectrobe."

"You're right! But these are ancient, aren't they?" Rallen asked. "I mean, it doesn't make sense. The Spectrobes have been around a real long time and all, but still. This is really kind of unbelievable."

Jeena shook her head. "I don't know. You and I still know so little about the Spectrobes and the Krawl . . . it's interesting," she said, running her fingertips across the carved runes. "Seems like a pretty comfortable relationship they had with Spectrobes."

She turned away and started investigating the rest of the ruins when something lying on the floor caught her eye. "Hey, this fragment. Look— it's glowing . . . red."

As they examined the strange glasslike fragment Komainu was poking around the rubble. Suddenly, he ran further into the cave.

"We're going to have to get a leash for him soon," Rallen grumbled.

"Maybe," Jeena said. "But not quite yet. Look what he found."

"Of course," Rallen said. "A fossilized Spectrobe."

"Hey," Jeena asked tentatively. "Is that Zeni? I bet he'll come in handy."

"Impressive," Rallen said approvingly. "You've been studying your Spectrobes."

Jeena shrugged. "Studying is what I do. That and Aldous gave me a list of various Spectrobes he has come in contact with on his journeys."

"Oh, that Aldous. A bag of information," Rallen mocked. "Well, this little guy looks funny," he said, looking down at the fossil.

"I know!" Jeena yelled. "That green shell and orange claws? And the round eyes? He so totally does! Then again, so do you. The difference? He's also cute."

Jeena picked up the fossil in one hand as she balanced the red Shard in the other.

"Here, let me give you a hand," Rallen said,

reaching out to grab the fossil. But the moment his hand made contact with it, the world around Rallen melted away . . . and another world appeared.

He seemed to be looking out through someone else's eyes. It was from a much lower point of view, meaning that it was someone either much younger or much shorter, or both. Or perhaps he was sitting down? Rallen tried to move his head to look at himself, but he wasn't able to control the viewpoint. Instead, he decided to try to take in as much information as possible from what was being presented to him.

He soon realized that the vision he was experiencing took place here on Wyterra; in fact, he recognized the Tree of Life. There were two people talking. With a shock, he saw that one of them was the older woman who'd been so rude to them earlier . . . only she wasn't older at all, and she was happier than when they last met her.

She was talking to a young man with long orange hair. Although he was perfectly calm, something about him radiated power, and Rallen—or whoever's eyes Rallen was looking out of—could tell that he would be formidable at whatever he chose to do.

The man's eyes were closed, and he seemed to be reciting a poem:

"Minions of doom, gathering
    strength,
Threatening all with eternal
    night
Until the One upon whom we wait
Encounters the invincible beast
    of the light. . . .
The slumbering Beast-King
    will once again stir.
Rising with him: the vagabond,
    prophesying peace;

And after his destiny's surely
    fulfilled,
Retiring again where no living eye
    sees . . .
Five far-flung worlds—
Five separate beds cradle his
    war-weary bones
As he gravely awaits the dreaded
    summons
Of the next clashing swords
    and the next battle
    moans. . . .
Abandoned we're not,
Yet his absence aches in us,
    as if hope itself were cut
    mortally deep.
Oh, cruel Victory!
Why must it be that in winning,
We must lose our great savior
    to another long sleep?

The man paused and took a deep breath. "Five sites," he said softly. "Five different resting places. And one of them happens to be right here . . . in these ruins." He looked toward the floor. "All this can only mean one thing: the Shards of the king—or the 'bones'— are scattered in ruins on five planets. But there's something critical I don't know yet . . . this Beast-King—exactly what kind of being is it?"

The man fell silent. Then, opening his eyes, he stared intently at the woman.

"You're an intuitive type, Gretta: what do you think?"

Gretta started to speak. "Uh . . . me? Well, uh . . . it's hard to . . ." She shrugged. "Um, I sup- pose . . . uh . . . why me, anyway?"

The man shook his head. "No, no—you're thinking. Don't think. Just . . . let your heart blurt out an answer."

Gretta frowned. "But I have no idea. I mean, even my heart has no idea." She paused, then added hesitantly. "Except maybe . . ."

"Yes?"

"I don't know, really . . . It's just . . . I think we should leave the Shards alone. I mean, they're at peace. *We're* at peace. It's just—my *heart* feels—that there's just too much risk." She shook her head again. "I don't know. Tell me, Master: what do *you* think?"

He laughed softly. "I think you're very wise for your age."

The man gazed off into the distance. When he spoke, it seemed to be to himself as much as to Gretta. "It's true. The poem clearly implies that this thing should only be summoned . . . in *very* dire circumstances."

The vision faded, and when Rallen blinked, he saw Jeena looking at him with worry in her eyes. "Rallen! Hey! You there?"

"Yeah . . ." he said, slowly getting his bearings. "Yeah, I'm . . . Jeena, did you see any of that?"

Jeena took a step back. Rallen recognized her skeptical expression as she tried to figure out if he was serious or not.

"Any of what?" she asked.

"No, listen, seriously—I just had the weirdest thing happen." Rallen groped for the words to explain it. "When I touched that Spectrobe fossil, I experienced, like, a, I dunno . . . a vision? Or something like that."

To his immense relief, Jeena nodded. "Yeah, you totally zoned out there. So . . . what did you see?"

"Well, first of all, this is going to sound crazy, but . . . I think I was looking through the eyes of a Spectrobe. In fact, I'd guess I was seeing what this little guy saw," he replied. "Let's get out of here. I'll tell you on the way."

"The way?" she asked, following his lead. "Where are we going?"

"Back to the village," Rallen said, grimly grabbing the red Shard on the ground and tucking it away in his satchel. "We're going to find Gretta . . . and tell her what we found."

CHAPTER SEVEN

Gretta wasn't hard to find. The village was not very large, and *everyone* knew Gretta.

Her face clouded over when she saw Rallen and Jeena again. But this time it was they who caught her off guard.

"Gretta," Rallen said, showing her the red fragment, "look—here. A *Shard*."

Her eyes widened. "Good heavens . . ." she whispered.

"You recognize it," Jeena said.

Gretta nodded. "I do. I remember. Now I remember! It's all coming back to me! But . . ." She squinted down at the Shard. "It's been so long, but . . . but something's different about it."

"Like what?" Rallen said softly.

She shook her head slowly. "Might be a trick of the memory, but it just seems like maybe the glow of it wasn't quite as bright then as it is now.

"What does it mean?" she asked. But Rallen and Jeena could only shake their heads.

"So. What now? What does the glow mean?" Rallen asked, as they made their way back toward the ship.

Jeena shrugged. "I have no idea. I kind of thought I was getting used to never quite under-standing what was happening. But I'll tell you, even by *our* standards; this has been one per-plexing mission."

As they drew within sight of the ship, they could hear the sound of someone sending a message. Jeena sprinted to activate the com-link.

"NPP headquarters. Harry speaking."

"Hey! It's the new guy, Harry!" Jeena yelled.

"Jeena—is that you? Oh, it's great to hear your voice! You guys okay?"

"Of course we are," Jeena replied.

"Sure," Rallen muttered. "Practically a day at the beach."

"We were all worried sick," Harry said. "So where *are* you, anyway?"

"You . . . you don't know?" Jeena paused. "That's weird. Harry, are you saying Commander Grant hasn't circulated an update on us?"

"Huh," Rallen said softly. "I wonder . . ."

"Jeena?" Harry said, his image fading out briefly. "Jeena—you reading me?"

"Uh, yeah, roger that," Jeena swiftly replied. "Hey, is the commander around?"

"Negative. Sorry guys," Harry stated.

"Any idea when he'll be back?" Jeena asked,

trying to keep her voice light. If Commander Grant hadn't told anyone about their mission, there must be a reason for it, she decided. No use telling Harry that they were in another system if the commander didn't want it known. But the thought made her uncomfortable.

"I dunno," Harry said. "Actually, I was kinda hoping you could tell me. I haven't seen him at all since you guys left."

"That's odd."

"Yeah. He was acting, well . . ." Harry sounded concerned. "Frankly, sorta strange at the time. Probably because of that sector coming up again . . ."

"What? Sector? Harry, what do you mean?"

"Uh . . . you gotta keep this between us, okay?" Harry said, his voice growing quieter.

"Promise," Jeena said. "Nanairo ice-cream sundaes for a year if it goes beyond this conversation."

"Ooh! Really? I LOVE those things!" Harry yelled. Then, looking over his shoulder, he said in a quieter voice, "Okay, so here's the story. It seems that about thirty years ago, a young NPP officer disappeared on assignment out there."

"'Disappeared'?" Rallen echoed.

"What?!" Jeena yelled. "Really?"

"Hey!" Harry shouted. "Not so loud!" Then it seemed to occur to him that he wasn't being terribly stealthy himself. "Look, I want you to know I strongly recommended calling you guys back in, but I don't know, he just . . . he wouldn't."

"Harry . . ." Jeena said slowly. "Who was the officer who disappeared?"

"Okay. You sitting down? They're saying . . . it was Grant."

"*What?!*" Jeena and Rallen yelled at the same time.

"*Waaaait* a second," Rallen said, holding something up. "Harry! Is this *his* old badge?!"

"Huh? Rallen?" Harry's image faded again, but this time it didn't come back. "I'm not reading . . ." All they heard next was a burst of static—and then silence.

"Well," Jeena said finally, "how's your day going?"

Rallen had to grin. "Oh, it's just getting less and less boring by the moment."

"Hey," Jeena said. "What do you think about going and asking Radese what the deal with the glowing Shard is?"

Rallen shrugged. "Seems like as good a plan as any."

Radese's reaction was not what they'd hoped for.

"I . . ." he said, his eyes wide. "Oh, merciful heavens . . ."

"So . . ." Rallen said. "That's . . . not good?"

Radese didn't smile. "This glow—see it? The red glow? It's . . . it's an unmistakable omen of impending doom."

"Like . . . what kind of impending doom?" Rallen pressed.

Radese was not swayed by Rallen's attempts at humor. "The worst—*Krawl*. That's what this glow means."

"Maybe—" Rallen began.

"No," Radese said firmly. "There's no doubt about it. The Shards have always warned us when the Krawl were massing. But . . . this." He shuddered. "This is frightening even to me. I've . . . I've never seen a Shard glow with this intensity."

"Okay," Jeena said. "What should we be expecting? It's bad; we get that. But can you give us some sort of idea as to what's going to happen, and when?"

Radese shook his head. "I'm sorry to have to say this to you, but the truth is . . . I don't think our minds can begin to grasp the scale of the disaster that's facing us."

CHAPTER EIGHT

Rallen and Jeena made their way to Kogoeria, a campground where Gretta mentioned they might find Kamtoga.

"Well, it's beautiful, at least," Rallen said, looking up at the purple sky. Even as the snow fell, a billion stars twinkled brilliantly.

"If you like snow and cold," Jeena replied.

"More of a beach person?"

"Less of a frostbite person," she admitted. "Not that I was crazy about Genshi, either—a little lava goes a long, long way." She looked around. "Yeah, okay—other than being deadly cold, it is kinda beautiful here. But if you don't hate the idea of getting someplace warm—I wouldn't object to checking out that cave over there," she said, pointing to a spot a few dozen meters away.

They stopped at the mouth of the cave. "Not the first ones to check this joint out, are we?" Rallen said.

"Nope," Jeena agreed, shining her light on a jumble of tents, some of which had plates of food outside them. By the steam rising off of the plates, it was clear they hadn't been sitting there long.

"But now?" Rallen said. "No one. What's the deal here? Where is everybody?"

"It *is* strange. And by the look of things, wherever they went they left in one big hurry."

"Krawl ambush would explain it," Rallen suggested.

"Yup," Jeena agreed.

"Sure is quiet. Hope that doesn't mean . . ."

"Look," Jeena said. "Don't even . . . Let's just . . . Let's look around some more."

"Yeah . . ." Rallen said. "I don't think we're gonna have a chance to do that. Company."

Jeena turned around to see a Krawl between them and the mouth of the cave. "Ew," she said.

"Yeah, lovely critter, isn't she?" Rallen said, regarding the spiky blue and purple creature; it almost looked as if it was made of ice.

"How do you know it's a she?" Jeena replied.

"You know me," he grinned. "I've got a way with the ladies. Let's do this—*iku ze!*"

Without even stopping to think, Jeena mirrored Rallen's actions and assumed an attack position. Summoned by the Spectrobe Masters, Komonatu appeared.

On Rallen and Jeena's command, the Spectrobe, rushed the Krawl. But for some reason, his attack wasn't as effective as usual. The

Krawl was emitting blasts of fire. Komonatu was able to dodge them, but it wasn't easy; and his own attacks weren't doing any good.

"Rallen!" Jeena yelled. "What's the deal?"

"I don't know!" he shouted back. "Let's see if we have any more success."

Swallowing her fear, Jeena followed Rallen's lead. But their parries and thrusts did no more damage to the Krawl than Komonatu's attack had. They tried again and again, constantly having to fall back only to attack again, all to no avail. The Krawl continued to send out blast after blast as it stalked closer and closer to the officers.

Jeena was in excellent shape, but she was beginning to wear out. "What's the deal?"

"Got me," Rallen admitted. "It just shrugs off everything we throw at it . . . I'm running out of ideas." Jeena noticed that, while he wasn't nearly as tired as she was, Rallen was breathing hard and shiny with sweat.

"Uh, Rallen," she said hesitantly. "Maybe we better . . ."

"No way," he said firmly. "This *can't* be happening."

"*Try this.*"

Rallen and Jeena whipped around. There was no one there, but something said, "Insert these into your Cosmolinks—and hurry!"

A pair of cubes came hurling out of the shadows. Jeena and Rallen snatched them from the air. Jeena looked at Rallen with raised eyebrows.

"We got a choice?" Rallen said, inserting the cube.

Jeena did the same, and instantly large hologramlike shields sprang up from their Cosmolinks—and just in time. A blast of fire, which would have fried Jeena to a crisp, hit her shield . . . and was repelled back toward the Krawl. "Excellent!" she shouted.

Rallen rushed the Krawl, which tried sending a

fire blast in his direction. Rallen thrust his shield forward to meet the flames, and the blast ricocheted back onto the Krawl. The beast screamed as it retreated. A moment later, it was gone.

Jeena took a deep breath and held it a moment, before exhaling forcefully. She looked over at Rallen, who gave her his normal grin.

"Barely broke a sweat."

"Yeah, right," she said. "We were in big trouble before those cubes practically fell from the sky."

"And speaking of . . ." Rallen said, turning toward the sound of footsteps. A group of men stood there, but there was no doubt who the leader was.

The man in the center was quite a bit older than Rallen and Jeena. His weather-beaten face and graying hair belied the fire in his eyes.

Rallen said, "Thanks for the hand . . . Mister . . . ?"

The man just laughed. "Well, well. Look at you—you're practically schoolkids."

Jeena would have been more annoyed with the comment, but she could feel Rallen bristle next to her, and that helped her stay calm.

The man added, "Still, lots of heart, and goodness knows you can't teach that. You might want to polish up some of your battle skills, though."

"Just who the heck are you?" Rallen growled.

The man just laughed. "Easy there, tiger. A little respect for your elders. But, to answer your question: the name's Kamtoga. And thirty years ago, believe it or not, I was the one wielding that Cosmolink you're holding in your hand."

"Kamtoga!" Jeena said.

"Oh, hey, how are you?" Rallen replied with what Jeena could tell was forced nonchalance. But his casual greeting, Jeena could see, had an effect on Kamtoga—though whether he was impressed or annoyed, it was hard to say. "We've been looking for you. You used to live on Wyterra, right?"

Kamtoga paused. "I did," he said finally.

Jeena and Rallen waited for him to continue, but the silence merely stretched out. "Right . . ." Rallen said at last. "Okay, uh . . . listen, can you point us in the direction of any ruins around here?"

Again, Kamtoga paused, then he said, "Yes."

"Okay . . ." Jeena responded. "And can you tell us where they are?"

"Sorry, I'm afraid I can't do that for you," Kamtoga replied.

"Why not?"

"Lots of reasons, but mostly because it's extremely dangerous."

Jeena was about to respond, but Rallen jumped in suddenly, as angry as she'd ever seen him.

"Dangerous for me, you mean? Look, you saw me thump that Krawl!"

Kamtoga nodded. "I had a front-row seat for the action."

"Then quit patronizing us!" Rallen said. "Just tell us where the ruins are!"

Kamtoga exhaled heavily. "Here's the point: courage isn't courage if it's heedless. And if you can't understand that—and from just watching you fight and talking to you, I don't get the impression you do—well . . . all the more reason for me *not* to tell you where the ruins are."

"Whatever," Rallen snarled, throwing up his hands. "We'll just find them ourselves. C'mon, Jeena."

"Wait! Rallen . . . ?" Jeena said as her partner stalked off into the snow. She turned to Kamtoga. "Sorry. He . . . he means well. He's just . . . you know, sorta bullheaded sometimes."

For the first time, Kamtoga flashed what seemed to Jeena to be an authentic smile. "Yep. I know the type."

CHAPTER NINE

"Rallen. *Rallen!* Rallen!"

Although he'd left the cave barely half a minute before she had, Rallen was already disappearing from her sight. He hadn't reacted the first two times she called—whether because he couldn't hear her or was trying to ignore her, she wasn't sure—but the third time there was a slight hitch in his step. He only paused a moment before continuing, but his pace wasn't quite as rapid.

Jeena caught up with him. "Hey, what's the deal?"

"What do you mean?" he said, cutting angry eyes her way. "You heard that guy. He's a jerk. And if he's not going to trust us, well, fine! I'm not going to beg."

"Whoa, Rallen, hang on. Yeah, he wasn't the most helpful, but—"

"But what?"

Jeena tried to rein in her own annoyance. "But he did give us those shields."

Rallen didn't respond. They walked on in silence. "Yeah," he said after a minute. "That's true."

Jeena looked around. The landscape was desolate, just ice stretching as far as the eye could see. Huge, jagged crevasses cut across like scars, uneven, unpredictable.

"Rallen," Jeena said slowly, "I've got a bad feeling about this route."

"Why?" he replied with anger in his voice, then shook his head. "Look, we're almost there. No way I'm turning back just to hear Kamtoga say 'I told you so.'"

"Oh, man," Jeena said. Her voice was louder than she'd intended, but it got his attention. "Rallen, look, please—don't make this an ego thing. Kamtoga knows the planet. He knows the risks. Maybe he's got a good reason for reacting the way he did."

"Yeah, right."

"Oh, come on!" she yelled. "Listen, you've . . . you've come a long way in just a few weeks. But you're not perfect, and you don't know every-thing. Just . . . just grow up."

Rallen turned toward her, and Jeena could read the surprise and hurt in his eyes.

But only for a moment. Before Rallen even had a chance to mask his feelings, the ice beneath his feet gave way with a tremendous crack. As he looked down, a hole suddenly appeared. He shifted his weight, trying to find safer ground, but the hole grew bigger. As Jeena watched in horror, Rallen's feet flew out from under him, and he plunged into headfirst the crevasse.

"Rallen!" she screamed. Then the crevasse exploded in size, and she was falling, too.

And then nothing.

Rallen opened his eyes, but he couldn't see anything. As his eyes began to adjust, he realized he was encased in ice, nearly unable to move. By shifting back and forth, he was able to give himself some room to maneuver. After a minute, he'd cleared enough space so that he could use his own momentum to free an arm. Once that was done, he was able to use it to push up his upper body, and then finally free his trapped legs. He stood and stretched.

"Stupid place for a crevasse," he said, then he

smiled. "Never thought I'd feel so good about being half-frozen and bruised and battered."

He looked up. "Jeena!" he called. "I'm okay. You see any way out?"

He paused, confused by the silence. "Jeena?"

Rallen looked around. "Oh, no," he said, turning his head from side to side. "Jeena? Jeena!"

There was a small pile of ice and rock behind him, and he whirled around. Jeena was slowly emerging from her own mound of ice. "Jeena!" he yelled happily.

She ignored him, brushing ice off her shoulders and shaking her head to get the snow out of her hair. Rallen walked over to her and helped brush off her back. She jerked away, and he pulled his hand back for a second, then resumed clearing the ice. This time she let him help.

"Nice route you picked, partner," she said, cracking her neck and wincing from the pain.

"You're right, you sure knew what you were doing."

To her surprise, he looked contrite. "Yeah," he agreed. "My bad. Sorry."

She raised her eyebrows. As long as she had the advantage, might as well see where it went. "And . . . ?"

"And . . ." he said. "And Kamtoga . . . *might* have, sorta, had a point. I may be in over my head. A bit."

Jeena blinked. This was way more than she'd really expected to get. "Wow. Are . . . are you all right? Let me check your head. . . ."

"Yeah, yeah, I know." Rallen grinned. "Humility's still on my to-do list."

"Actually," she said, "I'd say you're getting there. And speaking of—how do you suppose *we* get out of *here*?"

"I expect I'll be able to help with that," a voice from above said.

They looked up. "Kamtoga!" Jeena said.

"Great," Rallen muttered. Jeena looked at him quickly, and he rapidly corrected himself. "I mean, *great*!" he said, breaking into an obviously fake smile.

Jeena sighed. "It's a start."

CHAPTER TEN

Kamtoga thought he might have a piece of rope long enough to reach them.

"No hurry!" Rallen called as Kamtoga went to fetch it. Jeena had to turn away to hide her smile. Despite herself, she was impressed: the sentence could be interpreted as accommodating or sarcastic, depending upon how well you knew the speaker.

Something caught her eye. "Hey," she said, "is . . . is that another Shard?"

They moved closer. "Sure looks like it. And look, another fossil!" Rallen said with excitement. "I can't wait to get him back to the incubator so he can grow. And speaking of growing, once Zeni turns into Zenigor and joins Komanoto in battle, we're going to be unstoppable!" Rallen bent over to pick up the bulky fossil. "Do you think—"

He stopped speaking and his eyes went blank. "Rallen?" Jeena said. "You okay?"

But he was gone again.

Rallen found himself looking up from a low vantage point. He was dimly aware that he was again seeing something from the past through the eyes of a Child Spectrobe who had been there.

There was a body lying facedown nearby. He moved closer.

"No!" a voice yelled. Rallen saw the man from Wyterra—the one who was in his earlier vision—run over and kneel next to the body. The man turned the body over and felt for a pulse. "Kamtoga!" the man yelled. Rallen realized he was looking at a much younger version of the Kamtoga he knew.

"Kamtoga!" the man yelled again. "It's me! Hey—can you hear me? Come on. Come *on*. Don't you skip out on me now."

Kamtoga's eyes fluttered, and he tried to sit up. With a groan, he sank back down again. "U-ugh." He moaned, then began to laugh weakly. "Heh-heh. Sorry, buddy," he said hoarsely. "Guess I really screwed up this time. . . ."

"Hey," the other man said, a hand on Kamtoga's chest to make sure he didn't try to rise again. "Shh—don't exert yourself."

The man's face grew grave,

almost angry. "But *do* listen up, you—you have *got* to start reining it in, you hear me? You're too impulsive. And it is going catch up with you."

The man turned away suddenly, hiding his face from Kamtoga. But Rallen—or the Spectrobe—could see that he was choking back tears.

Even without seeing his face, Kamtoga could tell how upset the man was from the way his shoulders slumped. "Hey. *Hey.* I'm . . . I'm sorry."

The vision faded, and Rallen found himself staring into Jeena's worried eyes. "Hey."

She stopped holding her breath and punched his shoulder. "I hate when you do that." She frowned. "Well? What'd you see this time?"

"Believe it or not, I saw Kamtoga. Only he was really young. And I saw the guy from the other time. And they seemed to be . . . well, I guess, partners."

"Yeah?" Jeena replied. "They get along about the same way we do?"

"Actually," Rallen said, nodding, "yeah, pretty much. The other guy thinks—or, I guess, thought—Kamtoga was too, uh . . . impulsive."

Jeena burst out laughing. After a moment, Rallen joined her.

"Glad you guys are having a good time," Kamtoga called down. "I got the rope. Should I leave you down there for a bit? Or are you about ready to come up? You can take your time and think about it, if you want."

"That's okay," Jeena called up. "You know us—we tend to make snap decisions." She eyed Rallen, who just shrugged.

The look on Kamtoga's face made it clear he couldn't understand why this sent them off into gales of laughter again.

*T*he first thing Rallen did after he and Jeena had escaped the crevasse was to offer his hand to Kamtoga.

"Thank you," Rallen said. The older man looked skeptical, so Rallen added, "Really. I mean it. You saved our lives. And . . . and I was a total jerk before. I apologize."

Rallen's gratitude threw off Kamtoga. "Oh, well, uh . . ." he stammered. "Forget it. Never happened, all right?"

Rallen shook his head. "But it did happen. And you did save us. I may be a Spectrobe Master, but I obviously still need to master myself."

"Mmm." Kamtoga nodded, and his gaze grew distant. "That . . . that isn't exactly easy—take it from me. But realizing you've got a problem— well, that's half the solution. Because at the end of the day, teamwork's our best hope for getting rid of these monsters. And if teamwork doesn't come naturally—and to some folks, it doesn't—well, then we have to train ourselves for it."

"How do you do that?" Jeena wondered.

Kamtoga shrugged. "It takes time. And the

whole thing has to start with investing all you've got in the one closest to you—your partner. And I'm speaking from experience," he added. "I had a bond like that once. . . ."

"What do you mean?" Rallen pressed. "What happened?"

"He . . ." Kamtoga seemed to be groping for words. "He is no more."

Jeena and Rallen looked at each other, troubled.

"**M**an," Rallen said, gazing at his ship as if it were a drink of water being offered to him after a week on the lava planet, Genshi. "That's a sight for sore eyes, huh?" They had parted ways with Kamtoga some way back, after he had finally agreed to give them a list of planets in the system that had ruins. Now that Rallen and Jeena had a plan, they both realized they were feeling much better—less unsettled, more confident.

"Sure is," Jeena agreed. "Hey . . . why didn't you tell Kamtoga about your visions?"

Rallen shrugged. "I dunno. How do you start a conversation like that? 'Hey, I touched this Spectrobe fossil and had this vision where a younger you was injured because you'd acted without thinking, and your partner was really angry with you—and by the way, you're *really* old now!'"

Jeena laughed. "Yeah, that's not quite the way to do it. But I see your point, I think." She grew serious. "Rallen, what do you think the deal is with these visions?"

"I dunno," he said, shaking his head. He looked at the Spectrobe fossil Jeena was carrying. "It seems to happen every time I touch—"

When Jeena and the Spectrobe faded from his sight, Rallen knew he was in another vision. Although he couldn't control what he saw, he was getting used to these strange experiences.

He was looking at a spaceship which had obviously crash-landed. The pilot, Rallen realized, must have been either very lucky or very good, because although they were in the mountains, they'd managed to land on a relatively flat plain. There was a deep scar ripped across the plain, showing the ship's route—and judging by the length of the crater, they'd been going extremely fast. If anyone had made it out in one piece, it would have been a miracle.

The man from Rallen's earlier vision and Kamtoga were standing in front of the smoldering spaceship. Fire was still erupting from the tail section, and a breeze carried the smoke past them—but it also fed the flames.

"No one could possibly have survived that," Kamtoga said, grabbing the man's arm. C'mon—it's no use. Let's clear out before it blows."

"No," the mysterious man said, getting out of Kamtoga's grip. "I have to make sure."

"Don't be stupid!"

"Kamtoga, please!" the man begged. "There's still time. I'm sure of it!"

Kamtoga was about to respond, but the man didn't wait. He sprinted for the ship and disappeared into the smoke.

"I thought I was supposed to be the reckless one," Kamtoga said with a growl.

The Spectrobe must have followed Kamtoga's partner, because Rallen could see the mysterious man making his way through the smoke. "Yell if you can hear me!" he called.

Through the crackling flames, a voice could faintly be heard. "Here . . . !"

The mysterious man followed the voice. There was a young man with dark hair pinned under some debris.

"Okay, hold on," Kamtoga's partner said, trying to lift the twisted, red-hot metal. "I . . . can . . . do . . . this."

But he couldn't. Again and again he attempted to lift the wrecked machinery, to no avail.

"Forget it." The trapped man grunted. "Get out of here. This thing's gonna blow."

The mysterious man ignored him and continued pulling at the debris.

"Look, don't be a hero," the young man managed. "You tried your best. Now, go!"

"Save your breath," Kamtoga's partner smiled. "Don't worry about me."

"Get out!" the man pleaded.

"I will—with you."

"You're gonna get yourself killed. . . ."

"Stop worrying and just save your strength, all right?" Kamtoga said, emerging from the smoke. "We may need you to actually help us here instead of bossing us around." By Kamtoga's friend's relieved expression, it was obvious he'd been putting on a brave face.

"Now, listen up," Kamtoga continued. "Once

we get you free, we're going to have to really run. How are you at the fifty-meter dash?"

The young man from the wreck laughed weakly. "I'm usually pretty good. I can't swear I'll be at my best today—but if you get me out of here, I'll be able to hold my own."

"Good enough," Kamtoga replied.

"I knew you'd come to help," the mysterious man said quietly.

"Hey, someone had to make sure you didn't screw up," Kamtoga said lightly. "Okay, now—you both ready to do this thing? On my count: one, two, *three*!"

Working together, Kamtoga and his friend were able to lift the debris a few centimeters. "I got it." Kamtoga panted. "Grab him."

The mysterious man let go of the metal and pulled the injured man's arm. The pilot pushed with his leg and managed to slide free a second before the mysterious man's grip gave way and the debris came smashing down again.

"What do you say we get out of here?" Kamtoga's partner asked hoarsely.

As they reached the cockpit door, an explosion rocked the ship, throwing them clear. Another explosion blew the ship apart as they dodged the flaming wreckage.

"I'd hate to see the repair bill on that," Kamtoga said.

"Good thing I borrowed it," the injured pilot said, and he began to chuckle. Soon all three of them were rolling on the ground, their convulsive laughter echoing off the mountains.

"**Y**ou're back," Jeena said.

Rallen shuddered, then nodded.

"Well? What did you see this time?"

"I saw . . ." he said, then stopped. "I saw that strange guy from the earlier vision and Kamtoga again, both still young. But Jeena, there was someone else, too. And I think . . . I'm pretty sure it was Commander Grant."

"What?" she gasped. "But . . . no. Rallen, that *can't* be right."

"I know," he agreed. "But that's what I saw."

She bit her lip. "Come on," she said. "Let's try to contact NPP headquarters again."

"Jeena!" Harry's unmistakable voice cut through the interference on the com. "Is that you?"

"Harry!" she yelled. "Yeah, it's us. You reading me okay? I'm having trouble getting a clean signal."

"What's your location?"

Jeena laughed. "Kogoeria. Doldogo. You pick!"

"Kogoeria? Doldogo? Those are

new ones to me. Boy, you and Rallen—you guys never do things the easy way, do you?"

"Hey, no fair. This one's not our fault. Blame the wacky portal, not us. Harry," Jenna said, growing serious, "listen. Really weird things are going on here."

"Weird? You guys? You don't say."

"No, really—even for us this is strange. We actually met an old friend of the commander's out here."

"No way. You're kidding, right? I mean, how's that even . . ." Harry's voice faded. Jeena started to adjust the com, and his voice came back. "Oooh. Wait a minute—of course. From that time he disappeared, right?"

Jeena's mouth dropped open, but Rallen responded. "Exactly! Apparently, they were brothers in arms against the Krawl."

"So what's the story?" Jeena interjected. "Is the commander back yet?"

"Uh, well . . ." Harry began.

"Well, what?" Rallen prodded impatiently. "Come on, Harry—what's going on?"

"Look, there was a ship that took off without authorization," he replied.

"And?" Jeena prompted.

"Wait a minute," Rallen said slowly. "Harry . . . are you saying you think it was Commander Grant?"

"Look, I don't know . . . Yeah. Yeah, okay, I think it probably was him. I mean . . . there's a lot about this that doesn't make sense, right? Like sending you guys out there totally unprepared."

"What are you talking about?" Rallen said. "He'd never do anything like that intentionally."

A burst of static rang out. "Well, that's that— Harry's gone," Rallen said.

To Rallen's surprise, Jeena said softly, "Still . . ."

"Hey. *Hey*," Rallen said. "No. If we can't trust Commander Grant then . . . then *everything's* up for grabs. No. It's not like him. He wouldn't trick us." He paused, then added. "And . . . and if there is some reason he had to, I'm sure it's a good one."

"Okay," Jeena said, in a voice that wasn't quite as sure as Rallen wanted it to be. "You're probably right. . . ."

CHAPTER ELEVEN

*I*t felt good to be back in space. For a while, at least.

"Hmm." Jeena grunted.

"Is something wrong?" Rallen asked.

"Yeah," she said. "I'm picking up a weird transmission." She paused to listen. "I think it's a voice, but I can't really tell."

"That *is* weird," Rallen agreed. "Turn it up."

She cranked the volume. "Listen."

Rallen strained to make out words. Suddenly,

a high-pitched noise burst from the speakers. "Heeeeeeh! Heeeeeeh!"

"What is *that*?" Rallen said. "Besides creepy, I mean."

"Wait!" Jeena said.

"—body, ple—" The sound faded, then came back. "—eeelp! Heeeeeeelp!"

"Well, *that*," said Rallen, "we definitely recognize. Can you I.D. him?"

"I wish," Jeena said, frustrated. "But I think I can get a fix on it. And . . . wow. I mean whoever it is, it sure doesn't sound like they're faking, does it?"

Rallen shook his head. He was surprised to note that he had goose bumps. "That's for sure," he said.

ellow?"

"Yellow," Jeena agreed.

They'd followed the distress signal and found

themselves orbiting a planet which was yellow as far as the eye could see. Yellow sand under a yellow sky, broken up by giant yellow-brown boulders.

Rallen landed on the edge of an enormous crater. "This," he said as the ship touched down, "is my new favorite crater."

"Did you have a previous favorite?"

"No," he admitted. "But if I *had*? This would beat it."

They exited the ship. Jeena held up her kaylee, trying to pinpoint the distress signal.

"This guy couldn't get lost on a nice beach somewhere?" Rallen muttered. "The crater's impressive and all, but this heat is enough to make me miss Wyterra."

"Not me," Jeena replied, trying to get her bearings. "You almost drove me crazy with your constant complaining about the cold there."

"Me? No way." Rallen scoffed. "I never

complain. I'm just saying we better find our guy soon, 'cuz I'm turning into a baked potato here."

Jeena held up a hand. "Wait—hear that? It's a voice! Someone's calling to us . . ."

Over the sound of the shifting sands, they could faintly hear what sounded like someone calling for help. Jeena rushed to the edge of the crater and looked down. "Someone's trapped down there!"

"Hey!" Rallen called "Down there! Can you hear me? We're here to get you out. Are you hurt? What's your condition?"

"I'm . . ." the voice was barely audible above the wind and shifting sand. "I'm alive."

Rallen rolled his eyes. "You don't say."

He ran back to the ship, grabbed a rope Kamtoga had given them, and secured it to the ship's winch. "Wish me luck," Rallen said, disappearing over the side. A few minutes later he called up, "Jeena! I've got him! Pull us up!"

* * *

"**S**o, Neal, is it?" Jeena asked, standing over the odd figure they'd rescued. "Are you all right? Take a breath. It's okay—you're safe now," she said in a comforting voice. "How long you figure you were down there?"

Neal laughed tiredly, rubbing at his blue-green goggles as though they were eyes. "Oh, well . . . a while. No big deal, though. Happens all the time."

"It . . . it does?" Rallen asked.

"Sure." Neal shrugged. "All part of the job if you're an explorer."

"Really. And you don't mind?" Rallen asked.

"Not really. Getting trapped in tunnels and traps and stuff is . . . well, it's sort of what I do. True story—this is good. I once popped a piton on

114

a climb—a mountain climb—about a month ago . . . maybe a couple of years. Don't remember. Anyway, I spent a whole week dangling from a cliff in a raging blizzard." Jeena and Rallen stared as Neal began laughing happily.

"Well, I guess this was nothing, then," Rallen said. Jeena could tell he was grumpy because his rescue hadn't been properly appreciated. "Good thing there are people willing to help you out when you screw up."

"Yeah," Neal agreed pleasantly.

"So . . . how'd you get trapped down there?" Jeena asked.

"How . . . ? I . . . uh," Neal looked down, confused. "I . . . don't know, really . . ."

"What do you mean you don't know?" Rallen said.

"What's the last thing you remember?" Jeena prompted.

"Thing . . . ? I. Oh. I . . . well it could have

been that . . . that mechanism I was . . . you know . . . messing around with. . . ."

"Mechanism?"

"Yeah, man, it's this kind of an intricate lock system, you know? And I was messing with it."

Jeena and Rallen looked at each other. "Thank you, *man*," Rallen said. "You're very helpful."

"Could you show us where it is?" Jeena asked.

"Oh, yeah, that's totally no problem whatsoever," Neal said. "It's in the ruins."

Fortunately, the ruins were easy enough to find.

"So this is it—the famous mechanism," Rallen said, looking at the object. "And I guess this is the last lock of the famous mechanism?"

"Ooh! Ooh!" Neal said joyfully. "Isn't this just the most awesome of all awesome things? See, this is why exploring old ruins is, like, the coolest thing in the whole omniverse!"

"He's like a six-year-old," Jeena said to Rallen.

As if to prove Jeena's point, Neal called out, "Let me unlock it! Can I, please? Please, please, please, please, please?"

Jeena looked at Neal coldly. She'd been amused by him at first, but even a short time in his presence had cured her of that. "No," she said flatly.

Neal pouted. "But why *not*?"

"Basically," Rallen replied, "she's saying this is sort of a Rallen job, Neal."

"No," Jeena corrected. "What I'm saying is: I've got it."

"What?!" Rallen said. "Jeena! But *why*?"

Jeena laughed. She was pretty sure—but not positive—that her partner was imitating Neal's whine on purpose. It distracted her from noticing that Neal had snuck behind them both and unlocked it himself.

Rallen and Jeena spun around, alerted by the sound of machinery starting up.

"I can't believe he just did that," Rallen said. Jeena thought she detected a note of admiration in his voice. "Get down!!"

Jeena hit the dirt immediately, pulling the clueless Neal down with her. The ground began to shake violently. Jeena rolled to the side as something emerged from the ground. All three continued to move away, searching for shelter, as the ground erupted around them.

"It's . . . it's incredible . . ." Rallen said.

Jeena had to agree. Where just minutes before there had been nothing but ruins, what Jeena could only think of as a fortress now stood.

"Wow," she said. "It's just . . . I mean, the things that can be right under your feet without you even knowing it."

"Awesome, right? I told you, didn't I?" Neal panted. "I said it was going to be awesome and look—awesome! Right? Can I call 'em or can I call 'em? I mean, it's totally . . . it's huge! No one's ever—I mean, in the history of the whole . . . We're gonna be totally famous!"

"Well, I kinda already am." Rallen demurred.

"In your own mind doesn't count," Jeena replied.

"Says who?" Rallen shot back.

"Those measly little ruins!" Neal continued, not even noticing the others. "Who would've thought! This is, like—it's mind-boggling! Look at it! Look at it! Ancient people did this! How? How'd they do it? How'd they think it? Did they think about doing it—or just do it?"

He finally turned to the others. "Geniuses, right? I mean, they had to be!"

He waggled his head happily. "I'd dangle from a thousand cliffs on a thousand planets in a thousand blizzards for a moment like this! Anyone would, right?"

"Hey," Jeena elbowed Rallen. "Is that another—"

"Sure is," Rallen said, walking over to the glowing red Shard which was also lying right next to a Spectrobe fossil. Knowing what was next, he reached out and touched the fossil—

And entered the vision. He was in a chamber which seemed to have some sort of ritualistic use—there was a large altar. The same mysterious man from the earlier visions entered, muttering to himself.

"This fortress was ground zero in the great war with the Krawl so many years ago," he was saying. "But it wasn't any defensive maneuver that finally turned the tide in the Ancients' favor. It was pure offense—the Ultimate Form Spectrobe."

The mysterious man paced more quickly, seeming to get caught up in what he was saying. "And it's said that only the threat of an unprecedented disaster can force the Ultimate Form to rise again."

He shook his head. "Our struggle with the Krawl grows more dire and desperate by the hour, and yet . . . there's still no sign. Hard as it is to imagine, there's only one possible conclusion— the worst is yet to come."

The strange man stopped and stood completely still for a long moment. Then he raised his head and spoke clearly. "I can either await that ending or act now to change the story."

He strode out of the chamber determinedly. Rallen expected the vision to fade, but to his surprise, it continued. He didn't understand why, until a figure stepped out from the shadows, where it had been unseen by the mysterious stranger.

It was Commander Grant. He had heard everything.

"*I*'m so confused," Jeena said.

"I know," Rallen replied. "Kamtoga,

Commander Grant, whoever that other mystery man is—they all knew each other back then. But what happened? How did Commander Grant get to the Kaio System? Why isn't Kamtoga a Spectrobe Master anymore? And who was the third guy—and where is he now?"

An alarm sounded, causing them both to jump.

"Hey," she said, "we've got an incoming call."

"Ahh! Finally! Good!" The voice came over the com loud and clear.

"Commander Grant?!" Jeena replied.

"Commander!" Rallen yelled. "Where in the world have you—"

"That can wait." Their commanding officer's reply was brisk. "There's a matter of far greater urgency to discuss."

"But, sir—"

"Rallen, you're going to have to trust me. Time is short. There's a new destructive device, a game-changer that Krux has deployed in deep space. And we've located it. It's on the move, and from what we can tell it appears to be locked on Wyterra in the Kaio System."

"Commander," Jeena said, "this weapon— what, exactly, do we know about it?"

"Very little at this point. It's reading as a single, giant mass of Krawl energy. And when I say 'giant,' I mean it. If this thing were solid, it would qualify as a planetoid—that's how large it is. Its aggregate destructive capability is in a class all by itself. It will destroy a whole planet upon impact."

He paused to allow this information to sink in. "This Krawlosphere is a threat like none that's ever been seen before."

"And it's targeting Wyterra?" Rallen asked. "But . . . why? What's their strategy? Has any intelligence come in on that?"

The commander didn't reply.

"Sir? Are you there?" Rallen asked. "Commander . . . ?"

He slammed his fist down. "Not again! Jeena—get him back! What's the matter with this equipment?"

"Well," she said defensively, although there was no way any of it could have been her fault. "It's not like this was designed for use in the Kaio System." She paused. "As far as we know."

Rallen shook his head. "Just when he could've told us something useful. Now what?"

CHAPTER TWELVE

"*N*ow, that's a tower."

Jeena and Rallen stood on the planet Slayso—the next on the list Kamtoga had given them. They leaned back, craning their necks as far as they could. The yellow monolith was gorgeous and huge, and there were alien inscriptions on it. Rallen thought it looked like what would result if a microchip designed a temple.

"You can't even see the top," he added, with admiration.

"It's amazing," Jeena said softly. "It has to be at least a mile tall." She paused, thinking. "I sure hope their technological genius included elevators." She shook her head. "I don't know about you, but I've never seen anything even remotely like this anywhere in the whole Nanairo Galaxy."

"Me, neither," Rallen agreed. "I'm guessing they built it after the original Krawl War, way, way back. But . . . but why would you ever want to build a monumental thing like *this* on such a desolate planet? I mean, Slayso may not be Genshi, but it sure isn't Wyterra either."

"Yeah . . ." Jeena looked around. "Good question. I guess it might make sense if what you *really* wanted was to be sure it would be preserved for posterity."

"You know what?" Rallen asked. "I'm starting to really love things like that." Jeena turned to look at him quizzically. "You know," he explained. "Historical mysteries. Really gives the ole brain a workout."

Jeena opened her mouth to tease her partner, then decided not to. Rallen still drove her crazy, but he really had grown up an awful lot in their short time together. "Come on," she said, starting forward. "Let's take a look inside. Sometimes a little physical exercise helps to figure these things out."

They found an enormous set of doors leading into the tower. Rallen reached for the handles, then stopped and turned to Jeena.

"What do you think? Locked?"

She considered it. "I think that would be more typical. So I'm going to say unlocked."

Rallen nodded and pulled the handles. The doors swung open easily.

They walked across the lobby, their footsteps echoing ominously. Rallen whirled around. The suddenness of his movement made Jeena jump.

"What is it? You okay?" she asked.

"I dunno," he replied. "Just . . . something. Can't you feel it?"

She looked around. Nothing seemed different, and there was certainly no sign of danger. And yet . . . she realized he was right. She *could* feel something. Something malevolent.

She shook her head. Was she imagining things? Was Rallen freaking her out? Or was she getting more in tune with things, the way he was? She looked more closely at the walls, but there was nothing she could see there. The floor? No—or if there was anything, she wasn't picking up on it.

Then she looked up. "Krawl!"

As if called by her scream, the Krawl dropped down in front of Rallen. Rallen, Jeena wasn't entirely surprised to note, smiled. "C'mon! C'mon!" he said softly yet intensely. "I'm ready! Bring it!"

He and Jeena raised their Cosmolinks. "*Iku ze!*" Rallen said.

Before they could jump into battle, a deafening

noise rang through the tower. It pierced their ears and caused them to crumple to the ground in pain. The sound lasted for a few more seconds and then stopped. They regained their senses and stood up.

"Got a theory?" she asked.

He shook his head. "Not really. But . . . check it out—the Krawl's not attacking. Why isn't he attacking? They *always* attack."

The Krawl had not only stopped attacking, it was no longer even moving. Rallen and Jeena also fell still, staring at it.

"Um," she said. "Got any theories *now*?"

"Maybe they've decided resistance is futile and they're giving up," Rallen suggested.

"Um, *riiiight*." Jeena said sarcastically.

The Krawl began moving backward, then turned and scurried off.

"Is . . . is it retreating?" Rallen asked in disbelief.

"It appears to be."

Rallen was confused." You ever see a Krawl retreat before?"

"Can't say as I have," Jeena said. "In fact, it's not *possible*. It's not in their DNA. That's the whole thing about them: they either kill their prey or die trying."

"Okay," Rallen said. "So . . . what do we have here? Different DNA? Which would mean . . . a new kind of Krawl?"

"That," Jeena said, "is just such a lovely thought. Maybe that piercing sound was like some kind of calling device? Perhaps they're regrouping for something."

"Or maybe it realized it was up against a Spectrobe Master," Rallen said coolly.

"You mean, *two* Spectrobe Masters." Jeena grinned.

Rallen smiled at his partner. He knew he had made a good choice in having her as his Co-Master. "So shall we continue on up?"

* * *

Jeena and Rallen staggered up the last few stairs. Jeena fell to her hands and knees, sucking in as much air as she could. Rallen took a few more steps and then almost collapsed himself, but managed to stay upright by grasping a low wall.

He blinked, sweat stinging his eyes. His vision was blurring from exhaustion, so it took him a moment to process what he was seeing. When he was able to, he gasped.

"Jeena, you've gotta see this—check out the view of Slayso from up here."

Jeena groaned but managed to get to her feet and make her way to the railing. When she did, she also gasped when she looked up and saw the planet glowing in the distance. "It's . . . it's so beautiful." She paused, thinking. "And informative. I mean, this solves the mystery of this tower's purpose right there."

"Huh?"

"It's a memorial," she explained. "It must be. It's the perfect place to gaze up at Menahat and remember all the casualties of that war."

Rallen smiled wistfully. "So why am I thinking of Kollin suddenly?"

"You're homesick?"

He shook his head. "Nah. It's not that. I mean, sure, I'd like to get back but . . . I just . . . I hope the same thing never happens there."

Jeena was silent, drinking in the view, and thinking of home—her coworkers, friends . . . parents. "Yeah. Yeah, me, too."

"Jeena . . ." Rallen turned away, as if to take in the view from a different angle. "You think it's going to? You think that *this* might happen to our system? I mean, the Krawl, they've . . . they've actually done even *worse* than this to other places."

"Yeah," she said. "I mean, yeah, they have, you're right. But no, I don't think this is going to happen to the Nanairo Galaxy."

Rallen turned toward her suddenly. She couldn't tell if he was angry or hopeful. "Why not? Why won't it happen to us?"

"Because," she said. Jeena looked down, then straight into his eyes. "Because we won't let it. I just wish we had some more help, that's all. I mean—"

"Jeena!" Rallen cried. "Look at your Cosmolink! It's glowing!"

"What does that mean again?" she questioned. "Sorry, still getting used to the Spectrobe stuff."

"Well, that means . . . Never mind. Hold it to the sky."

"Why?" she asked.

"Just trust me!"

Jeena nodded and threw her hand into the air. "Like this—?"

A dazzling light shot out from the Cosmolink and cascaded down to the floor, and a giant

creature landed just a
few feet away from
them. It had a hard
shell that resembled a
shield. Giant horns
grew from its back
and extended up,
their tips razor sharp. The creature's entire body
was covered in a beautiful green-and-yellow
colored armorlike skin. It moved slowly toward
Rallen and Jeena and bowed its head. Normally,
someone would run from such a strange and
enormous thing. But Jeena and Rallen knew that
he was a friend.

"Say hello to Zenigor!" Rallen grinned.

Though Jeena had seen several Spectrobes
before, they never ceased to amaze her. "Wow.
He's wonderful!"

"I know," Rallen said casually. 'I can't wait to
see him in action!"

All of a sudden, Rallen's Cosmolink began to glow brightly.

"Is it my birthday or something?" he asked jokingly. Rallen held his Cosmolink up to the sky and looked at his grinning partner. "Well, here goes nothin' . . . *Iku ze!*"

That same light that had come from Jeena's Cosmolink now poured out of his, causing Rallen and his partner to cover their eyes. When the light faded, they lowered their hands. Jeena then covered her mouth—in awe. There, in front of them, was the most magnificent Spectrobe they had ever seen. His massive physique was lean and sculpted, and two giant spiked rings were connected to his upper body. Two large fangs hung down out of his massive jaw. His blue and golden fur glistened like the stars in the sky. He resembled a fierce lion, king of his world.

"Okay, Zenigor is awesome . . . but this guy . . .

more awesomer." Rallen managed to squeeze the words out.

"Awesomer is not a word," Jeena said, unable to take her eyes off of this wonderful new Spectrobe. "I'm not sure I know his na—"

"Optoger," Rallen said in a serious tone. "His name is Optoger."

"How do you know?"

Rallen looked at his confused partner and simply said, "I study, too, ya know."

There were a few moments of silence as Rallen and Jeena took in their surroundings. With Zenigor and Optoger standing right in front of them—massive, strong, and beautiful—and the distant planet shining down on them and the wonderful tower they were standing in, Rallen and Jeena knew now was the time to put an end to the evil Krawl and save this galaxy and their own.

Rallen unleashed his laser sword. Jeena followed. Rallen stared at her with a serious expression, and then broke into the grin that had almost driven her out of her mind at first. Now she returned it.

"So, partner," he said, turning to Jeena, "shall we take care of business?"

She smiled, "If not us, who will?"

"Good point. Let's go find those last two Shards, shall we?"

"We shall."

Far away on the desolate deserts of planet Slayso, a dark figure stood.

"Children! And yet clearly not children. I underestimated them. No matter. They'll be food for sandworms soon enough. For they will know my name is Krux!"

Krux looked up to the sky and gazed upon . . . the Krawlosphere! It was dark, eerily mesmerizing. Its sheer size dwarfed anything on the planet. Yet Krux was calm and not intimidated by his evil creation.

"With my own dark power, I command you now to cease your selfish slumbers. Flay this planet raw! And all planets surrounding it! Fulfill the dreaded destiny denied you in ages past! Go! Go and destroy everything! Everything! Krux commands you!"

The Krawlosphere began to glow and growl as if alive, and in a flash of light rocketed out of sight.

And with that, Krux, too, vanished . . . leaving behind a dark laugh that echoed through the night sky. . . .

Not The End

THE STORY OF THE SPECTROBES CONCLUDES IN THE ULTIMATE RETURNS . . .

Rallen and Jeena continue their quest to find the last two Shards, which will unleash the Ultimate Form and put an end to their newest threat, the Krawlosphere. But with the Shards come more visions. What do Commander Grant, Kamatoga, and the mysterious man have in common? As the heroes try to find the answers, a familiar face from their past returns to finish what he started: Jado! Battles will ensue, friendships will be destroyed, and an evil past will be revealed. Will the Ultimate Form save Wyterra, or will Krux and his wicked force of light-eaters reign supreme and destroy the Kaio System? Find out what happens in *Spectrobes: The Ultimate Returns!*